the girl who couldn't come

JOEY COMEAU

First edition Spring 2011
Copyright © Joey Comeau, 2011

This is a work of fiction. I think. Names, characters, and places are the product of the author's imagination, or are used fictitiously, and any resemblance to actual persons, living or dead, is probably cause for nudity.

Printed in the USA

ISBN 1460920147
EAN-13 9781460920145

Cover by Joey Comeau
Design by Emily Horne and Joey Comeau
Edited by Derek McCormack
Drawing by Kate Beaton

This book is set in Baskerville.

for
FOURTEEN YEAR OLD JOEY

the girl who couldn't come

My problem is that I can't come unless Johnny Cash is playing. I can't orgasm without the sound of his voice in my ears. When I do hear him, I can't control myself. I'm afraid to drink in country bars because when they play a Johnny Cash song, I end up in the ladies' room with a stranger, straining to hear the music from the dance floor.

He doesn't even have to be singing. I heard him give an interview on the radio once, when I was eighteen. It caught me off-guard. His voice was just as powerful when he spoke.

"I wasn't all that high scholastically, because I was writing a lot of poems and stories and songs at the time," he said. Lying on my stomach in the living room, I found myself sliding back and forth against the carpet, my hand underneath me. "And I should have been studying more. But school was really important for me. And I was so disappointed in myself that I didn't make really good grades in math. In all the other subjects I did very well." The sound of him answering questions was as good as the albums I kept hidden under my bed. It possessed me, it wet me. I knew it was wrong, but I couldn't help it. His voice was rough sex. "But school was really important to me. My parents — my mother and father — I think they had an eighth grade education, which was adequate for what they did with their lives then. But they wanted me — and they drilled in me — I had to graduate from high school."

My mother came into the living room right when he was done talking, right at the beginning of a song. I didn't see her as the music swelled and I rubbed myself and came, my eyes closed and bunches of my pants clutched in my fingers. She stood for a minute as I rocked in time to the music, and she said "I don't know how you can listen this shit, honey. It's so rural."

It would be perfect if I could listen to Johnny Cash while I made love, but David doesn't seem to like it. He turns the CD player off before he comes to bed. And what can I say? Should I curl my fingers in his chest hair, press myself against him and whisper, "Please?" How do I tell him, "David, I can't come," without it being a big deal? Without him knowing that I've faked it. Without him being jealous. It isn't like I'm cheating on him.

Johnny Cash is dead.

And David is very much alive. He's been at the library all day, and he smells like old newspapers at dinner. While we eat he talks and talks about Neal Ball, who in 1909 turned the first unassisted triple play. I nod and I plan what I'm going to say, word for word. I have to tell him. But admitting sexual hangups to a man is never as funny in real life as it is in your head. In my head I say "Hey David, remember all those times I came when we *weren't* listening to Johnny Cash? Do you remember all those orgasms?" A pause for effect, and then, "About that." And what a great story that would make. Even if he left me, which I'm certain he will. It's a preemptive strike. Sure, I'm a pervert, but you can't even make a girl come.

Of course, it doesn't work out like that at all. I can plan and plan, but when we're sitting side by side on the edge of my bed, our clothes pulled open, all that comes out is mumbled nonsense. He has his cold hand up my front, tracing the wire of my bra.

David. Indie rock boy with the tight shirts and baseball card collection. David, who talks about sex using sports metaphors that are romantic instead of shallow, that turn sex into a game of heroes and legends.

David, who has never said, "This was so good, did you come, I came, did you really come?" Who has never said, "That was the best I've ever had." Who remembers sex as a series of plays, fouls, surprise victories and catches, describes them with veneration, his dark eyes intense, sincere. I can't bring myself to be cruel to him, even if I am scared, even if that's the smart thing to do. So it just spills out.

"It isn't you, it's me, I just can't, without, I mean, I love you, I love your body, and being with you is wonderful, and I don't even think he's sexy, you know, he's just got this voice that, it fills me up and I, it really isn't you, ever since I was a little kid I've been obsessed, you know? And it's the same with other men, it isn't just you." And as his brow furrows and he pulls his hand out from beneath my shirt, I say "I can't come unless we're listening to Johnny Cash." Then David is standing, pulling his pants up, fastening the button. He turns away, and it feels like my stomach is sucking in air.

But then he's putting on some music, smiling.

"Well," he says as the first trumpeting notes of the song fill the room. I want to say something but instead I close my eyes to the music, and he sits on the bed behind me. His legs wrap around me and he's lifting my shirt. "Love," he whispers in my ear, his voice soft as Johnny Cash fills the room, "is a burning thing." And it's working. It isn't Johnny Cash I'm hearing, but David. It's David's hands on my body. "And it makes." It's David fumbling at my skirt, pulling it down. I'm turning to his neck, his shoulders. Pulling his shirt off while he sings along, his voice a little louder now, "A fiery ring." He's watching me. "Bound," he says, "by wild desire." I've got his pants, pulling them down to his calves. He's got his lips against my ear, his breath hot. "I fell in," he says, "to a ring of fire."

one two three four five six seven eight

A woman picks him up. She pulls her car over onto the shoulder and looks at him out the passenger window for a minute before she lets him inside. She does let him inside, though, so he figures he doesn't look like a killer. He tries not to let it bother him.

While they drive, he counts telephone poles. While he counts, he adds secondary counts. Like, *one two three four (one transformer) five six seven eight nine ten eleven (two transformer) twelve*. Part of the game in his head is to see how many simultaneous counts he can keep going. Part of the game is acting like he's just staring out the window, thinking. Acting like a normal person.

He thinks about the family road trips he took when he was little. His father would try and get him interested in all sorts of games other than counting, but children can be stubborn. There was only one game he liked. Count all the cows on your side of the car. Count the trucks we pass. Count the telephone poles. It doesn't seem like a road trip without counting telephone poles.

The woman driving has blonde hair held up with bobby pins, and she lets it down after they have been driving for a while. It reaches down to her shoulders. It has a light of its own. She undoes the top two buttons on her blouse, casually.

"What're your plans in the big city, sweetie?" she asks, reaching her hand out to touch his arm. Her fingers are cool on his skin. He keeps counting. He is going to see his girlfriend. He thinks about the hill to her house while he counts. He thinks about the last time they had sex.

"Not much of a talker, huh?" she says. "That's okay. Just having the company on these long drives is nice." She smiles at him, and he counts telephone poles.

The next drive is better. An old man and his dog. No talking. Everyone's hair stays up. The drive is long and quiet, and he has time to think. The last time they were together, she told him, "Maybe this time we could focus on me a little more?" He didn't know what she meant. He shouldn't have gotten upset. He starts to get upset now, thinking about it, but that does no good. He tells himself, that does no good. Think about the solution.

It takes three more rides to get him to her.

It's not a big hill, but today is hot. It's been hot for the whole trip. Standing in the blistering heat on the side of the road, across from her house, all he thinks about is that one moment when she will open her mouth against his kiss and his hand will pull her tight. In the heat it is impossible for him to think of anything else. He touches the toe of his left shoe to the back of his right foot.

When she opens the door, she's surprised. She's wearing a tight button-up shirt. But he's focused on her eyes. He steps forward, puts his hand behind her head, and his fingers slide through the soft hair there. He kisses her mouth. He closes the door behind himself.

"How?" she says, but he kisses her again. Later he will lie. He'll say they let him out. Right now he holds both her arms right at the elbow and he squeezes. This is what he has been thinking about over and over. He wants to pull her toward him so hard that she breaks his skin with her whole body, so that they both break open and he's inside of her and she is inside of him. He kisses her neck, pressing hard with his tongue, moving up to her jaw line, beneath her ear. He touches his tongue to her ear-lobe.

She's wet with sweat already, from the hot day. She tastes like salt. They fall against the wall and his hands are at the top button of her shirt, trying to turn the button sideways, to slide it carefully through the hole. It is taking forever. She yanks at his hands, fumbling and then just tearing.

"I can sew," she says. She kisses him back now, pressing against him hard. She has her hands around his back. She pulls his t-shirt up and off. She kisses his nipple. Bites. He turns her around so that she's pressed against the wall, her shirt open and her bra and breasts against the wall. Her face is against the wall, mouth pressed open against white surface. He moves his hand down to her ass.

His fingers slide through sweat. They follow the line of her ass down, down and through her legs. His fingers pull and push at the zipper line of her pants, at the seam just on top of her cunt. The zipper is perfect under his fingertips. Interlocked. It feels so organized. So exact. He tries to touch each tooth of the zipper. *One two three four*, but she pushes back against him. He can't get distracted. Focus on her a little more.

He kneads her through the material and presses her into the wall harder and she pushes back against him. Her own hands undo the front of her pants. The zipper unzips. She pushes the pants down off her hips.

She's hot and wet and so his fingers slide over her easily, moving across wet skin and then back again. All of a sudden there is no pattern for him to hold onto. His hand is moving up and down and around in circles, but there is no structure for him. He closes his eyes. He starts to panic. He starts to count. He counts one for every time he moves his fingers. *One two three*

15

four five six seven eight. His fingers are sliding through and around and against her soft skin. The counting gives his movements structure. It calms him down. Four circles and then four up and downs.

Her face is turned around now, her mouth open, searching over her shoulder for his, and he leans forward to kiss her, his erection pressing into her ass through the front of his jeans, pressing her against the wall. His kiss is off the mark just slightly. He closes his teeth to make sure that he isn't counting out loud. In his head he is going, *one two three four five six seven eight, one two three four five six seven eight, one two three four five six seven eight.*

He presses one finger inside of her cunt and she starts to finger herself with him inside her. He slides it in slowly, and then pulls it out, one and then two, trailing the moisture along her skin, and then he moves the finger back to press into her again. He moves the finger in and out of her. One and then two.

"Two fingers," she says. So he slides two fingers inside, pressing against the walls of her. Then he slides them out. He grinds his cock into her ass in time with his fingers sliding into her cunt. He is counting slower now.

They are standing against the wall, but they are not quite close enough for him to touch the light switch. He bites her lip, first softly, and then harder. He pulls her with his teeth to the left. They lean. He reaches out and turns the light on. You can hardly notice the light in the room because of the sunlight from the window. He turns the light off again. His other hand is wet and he pushes two fingers inside her again. He realizes that he is counting out loud in her ear, "One two three four five six seven eight." She looks over to see him flicking the lights on and off in time with his count.

The surprise. The heat. The fingers inside her, moving with a mind of their own while she fingers herself, pressed against the wall. The cock pressing against her ass and his warm counting on her neck.

She comes. She comes, mouth open against the wall, eyes closed. In her head she is echoing him.

He wants to pull his own pants down and slide into her. She feels more open around his fingers, more relaxed. He wants to slide into place. He wants to turn her around so she's facing him, so her breasts are wet with sweat between them and so he can come inside her while he touches his finger to the left nipple first and then the right nipple. The left and then the right. But he waits for her. Her eyes are still closed and he waits for her to catch her breath.

ghosts

1.

In the hallway closet, the figure sat with a sheet over its head, three holes cut for a face. Two black holes for eyes. One black hole for a mouth. The sheet was white, and nothing underneath moved as I stepped forward. There was no sound. I undid my belt and pulled my pants down just enough. I put my cock into the mouth hole. It felt dry in there, too, like the soft rough feel of a new bed sheet. And it was warm, fresh from the dryer.

2.

In the middle of the night, I woke to chains in the stairwell. The figure again, trailing heavy locks and thick metal chains up and down the stairs. I watched from my bedroom door. The sheet was faint blue in the light. There were no eyeholes now, only one black mouth hole for its face. Another hole lower down on the front of the sheet.

I undid my belt again when it came close, the bottom of the sheet brown from carpet grime. I wrapped the heaviest trailing chain around the sheet, around the neck. I pushed my cock into the hole below the waist. There was no sound and then there was the rattle of the chain as I tightened it around the neck and then there was no sound. The hole was warm and dry around my cock.

I pushed into the black until I could feel myself coming. Then I pulled out and came on my hand, sitting on the stairs, almost changing my mind. But I pulled the chain around the neck tighter, and I used two fingers to shove my come into the mouth hole of that eyeless face.

3.

There were feet showing under the sheet. Thin, pale ankles, and small white toes. The front of the sheet was only two holes, still. And with the chains wrapped around the body, I could see the shape of her hidden breasts clearly. She was wet, now, and felt like flesh, but she was quiet. I brought my heel down hard on those small white toes, and she whimpered. I came on the top of her pale foot, where a dark bruise was forming.

4.

There were no holes in the sheet at all. She sat on the toilet, with the cover down. The bathtub was full already, with cold water. She stood up, and lifted the sheet to expose her pussy. She got down on her knees and leaned over the bathtub with the sheet still pulled up. I could feel her warm body. I took her hair in my fist through that sheet. I shoved her face into the water, and when I pulled her out again, I could see the shape of her jaw under the wet, clinging material. I shoved her head into the water again, and I fucked her harder while her sheet flowed and rippled and bubbled.

5.

I found her sitting in the kitchen without the sheet, smiling a wide, empty smile at me. I got another sheet from the hallway closet and covered her. Then I cut a hole in the back and I shoved her down. I pushed my cock into the black hole where I could feel her warm ass. She pulled the sheet off and turned to smile. Her eyes were all white now, like eggs, but she kept them half-closed, so it didn't matter. She licked her lips and sang my name, very quiet.

She sang my name, and then she sang the names of my childhood friends and my pets. I shoved my fingers into her mouth, and the nails on my hand scraped the soft skin inside. She tried to sing around my fingers. I pulled them out and shoved them into her mouth again. I fucked her face deeper and harder with my fingers each time, until she was choking her song. Until the only words in her mouth were my fingers.

6.

I walked all the way to the bathroom before I noticed the sound of chains. They were tied to my legs. I reached down to unhook them, but when I bent over, she pulled the chain around my neck, and her fingers pushed down inside the back of my underwear and against my asshole.

She lifted the sheet from my back, and she pulled my pants down and she pressed her tongue into me. I felt dry, even while she tongued me. Dry and warm.

7.

She wears my clothes. I know this, because she comes to the closet to put them in the hamper beside me. She tightens my belt around her waist. In the morning, she bites my sheet, and she takes it in her fist. She grabs the sheet that is my head and she leans against the wall of the closet and jerks off where my face used to be. She comes against the holes where my mouth and eyes should be.

the steps

The woman they send to landscape my lawn has mud all over the front of her tank top. She has a shaved head and from this distance her eyes are black like an animal's. There is a smear of brown dirt up the side of her neck. Her pickup truck is filled with tools, a lawnmower and three thin trees, each with a ball of dirt and roots wrapped in canvas at its base.

I watch her from the front step as she raises the pickaxe over her head and brings it down. I should be finishing my taxes. The deadline's today. But look at her. She isn't muscled, but she's strong. Her skin is tanned the color of wet stone. The ground comes up in chunks where the pick goes in. She lifts it again. I want to run my hands up her body when it is stretched out in that way. I want to push my fingers into her skin.

"Hey," I call to her, and she looks up. "Do you want a beer?" I say. She watches me for a minute, and I realize that she didn't know I've been sitting here, watching. She drops the axe on the ground.

"Yeah," she says, "all right."

I grab two beer bottles from the fridge inside and I can't help smiling. I wonder what her name is. I wonder whether she will let me run my fingers over her shaved head. I can already feel the bristles. My tax receipts are on the table by the door. There are discrepancies. The totals don't work. I need a break. I deserve a break.

I open the front door and step outside. I am smiling at her when I should be watching where I'm going. My foot catches, and I fall forward down the steps. There is no sound when my skull hits the cement at the bottom. It feels like someone is pulling very gently at my hair. The ground underneath my head is a stack of numbers, profit and costs and taxes and interest rates on loans. It scrapes at me. It trickles. There's something wrong.

I can see one of the beers pouring out next to me, and then I can see her kneeling down to peer into my face. I feel like suddenly all of the totals are matching. I hit my head too hard. She looks terrified. She shouldn't be. It all adds up. I lick my lips and reach out for her. The bristles tickle at my fingertips and her dark eyes go soft. I can hear her breathing now. Sound rushes back and I pull her toward me and we kiss. She rolls me over and it hurts like hell when her hand presses against my shoulder. She pulls at something and I feel faint. Her hand comes away with blood and a chunk of broken bottle and she tosses the glass and wipes the blood on her shirt.

This all feels right, like I am filling in boxes on a form. She straddles me and when she leans forward to kiss me again, I press up against her. I pull her shirt up to expose her breasts, my hand leaving dirt and my own blood on them. She bites my neck and she presses against me in return. She grabs my arm by the cut and squeezes and I feel like I am emptying. When she pulls her hand away and the pain is gone, I realize that she's undone my pants with her other hand. She wipes her hand through her hair, the dark blood streaking her shaven head.

She rolls off me, onto her back and pulls her pants down and off. I close my eyes and wonder whether my neighbours are watching. I wonder how much time has passed. She climbs onto me and takes my cock in her hand. She presses the tip against herself and slides it once through the dry hair and then down into wet folds of skin and back out through hair. She presses me through again, sliding me against and around the mouth of her cunt. I am tracing figures onto her hard stomach with blood and dirt.

She masturbates with me, pressing her forehead into my gashed arm and her breasts into my chest, breathing hard. She begins to rock against me, harder and harder, then she stops, pressing my cut harder and harder but not rocking and she says, "I'm going." The ground underneath me is still numbers but everything is numbers, the sky and the planets and every little atom in my body and I feel like I understand everything all at once. I feel peaceful and I think maybe I am dying.

She takes me inside her, slides down on me, her cunt wet and warm around my cock and she raises herself up again. She is a mirror in the sunlight. Her tank top is pulled up over one of her breasts, and I know that this isn't really happening, the way you know things in dreams. Her second breast is covered. There is blood all over her. She is dark like a forest.

christmas tree pornography

I lost my virginity at noon, which was too early in the day for a first time. I wanted to go to sleep immediately, but I knew I couldn't. It was the same strange sleepy feeling I felt when my father drove us into a tree. The paramedic knelt down and shined his light and said that I couldn't go to sleep, even though I wanted to. I had to stay awake for a few hours at least. Four hours, he said.

I lost my virginity at noon, which meant I couldn't go to sleep until at least four pm. I couldn't go to sleep and I couldn't talk to her. She was angry that we stopped and angry that I wouldn't make a deal with her. We sat until she went to the bathroom and I jumped to my feet. I found my sock. I found my two shoes. I got out on the street and I ran.

Arms out straight, fingers extended, I ran. The road ended and there were woods. My feet went between the rocks, through the leaves. They landed exactly where they had to. I kept running. I thought, "She's probably out of the bathroom," and I thought about her breasts with white triangles and dark centres and I ran a little faster.

My legs and arms and chest were burning but I couldn't stop. Inertia was on my side now. I would have run forever probably, except a man stepped out from behind a tree and said my name. I slowed down. I stopped. His tie had a snowman made out of flashing lights.

"Just give us a minute, Joey," he said. "We're still setting up." Behind him, two more men were trying to set up a big white screen. One of them was tall and handsome, dark hair with streaks of grey.

He looked professional. The other man was bigger and had red hair. Every time they unrolled the white screen, it rolled up again. Finally they succeeded.

"I love slideshows," the man with the tie said. The forest went dark and the white screen lit up. "Here we go." Click. The white square blinked away and came back as a photograph of me underneath her, my sock stuffed in my mouth, my eyes wild.

"That isn't the start," one of the men yelled. "Start at the beginning." Click. The screen went white again. Beside me, the snowman was still flashing in the dim light.

"In the beginning," the man said, "Joey and Daryl stole some rum." Click. Here was a photograph of my hand reaching out for a bottle of rum. "They went looking for a friend to drink it with." Click. Outside Samuel's house. "But Sam wasn't home." Click. Picture of Tina in the doorway. Her friend in the background. Click. Daryl pouring four drinks. Click. Tina pouring her drink down the sink.

"She filled it back up again with water," the snowman said.

"Get to the good part!" a woman in the darkness yelled. It was too dark to see anything now. It sounded like a crowded theatre. There were people murmuring. Someone coughed. I heard what sounded like static, big speakers above us where there should be only leaves and squirrels.

"Don't stop." Tina's voice. "I'll suck your cock if you promise to keep fucking me,"

The sound of me crying.

"That's not me!" I yelled.

Someone in the crowd was laughing. Now everyone was laughing. Click. Daryl and Tina's friend, her legs pushed above her head, both grinning. A cheer goes up. Click. Back to Tina. Her mouth on my cock. Click. Her lips are shining with spit. It trails to the tip of my cock through the air. Her mouth is open. Click. Reaction shot from my face. The crowd is laughing again. I can feel my face flushing with embarrassment. Beside me the snowman is still flashing.

Click. A condom rolled halfway down my cock.

A hand touches mine in the dark.

Click. The screen is white again, with a big dark spot in the middle. Her breast, close up. You can see the teeth marks on it. "Ow, shit," Tina's voice on the speakers. "What is the matter with you?"

The hand squeezes mine, pulls me close. Another hand touches my face. The snowman is closer now. Fingers slide through my hair, tighten, pull me down to my knees. The snowman comes closer, flashing, closer, and then he is gone and there's a cock against my lips. I open my mouth and lick.

"No," the snowman says. "Like she did."

I open my mouth and take it inside. Click. I can't see the screen anymore. There's more laughter, though. Click. A gasp of shock from the audience. When he thrusts into my mouth I can feel it pressing against me, deep. His fingers still hold my hair tightly. He controls my movement. All I can do is slide my tongue back and forth against the shaft of his cock. I'm hard. I have my own hand in my pants now, pulling myself off.

Click. Dead silence. I try to look, but I can't see anything. I can see the edges of the bright screen, through his public hair. I don't need to see. I'm full. I close my eyes again. Click. The speakers are still hissing a bit. I can hear a door slam and then the sound of feet pounding pavement. Click. The screen is brighter. He's bucking against me harder now.

Click.

When I get home my neighbours yell at me, they call me names but I keep my mouth shut. I haven't swallowed. His sperm is still in my mouth. My mother's watching TV behind the door. I go into my bedroom and I sit down to do homework. My books and binders are all over the bed. I can't concentrate on the math.

The phone rings and my mother calls my name.

I pick it up in the hallway outside my room. Tina.

"I'm sorry I laughed," she says. "Will you come back tomorrow?"

I don't say anything.

"Joey?" Tina says.

Nothing. I wait til she hangs up.

Later, when my homework is finished, I watch TV. I listen to music. I start to worry that it never happened. Maybe there were no people in the woods. Maybe there was no man with a slide projector. I put my hand out like a cup and I drool out the sperm. It's thick and white, mixed with spit now. I look at it for as long as I can stand it, and then I slurp it back into my mouth.

My hand is still damp, and I slide it down the front of my pants.

I'm hard again.

Under my bed, Tina is crying.

"Joey?" she says.

I don't say anything. She climbs out from under my bed and she lifts her legs up. There's no panties under her skirt. She has a fake cock tied to her with a grocery bag. "You don't have to look at me," she says. "You can just fuck me." One of her arms is sort of flashing, just under the skin. When I reach down to touch the cock, it lights up.

"Joey," it says. "Dinner."

and then the werewolf

In the park, we drink the wine right from the bottle and stretch out on our backs on the pine needles.

"You got any kids?" she says.

"No."

"I'm never having kids," she says. My fingers are cold, but when I touch her, she smiles again. I slide my hands across her stomach, so smooth and warm. I think about life growing inside, under my hand, and we stay like that.

She sits up and she pulls her sweater off. It pulls her under-shirt up with it, showing me the very bottoms of her breasts. I reach out and take the shirt in my hands and I hold it down as she pulls her sweater the rest of the way off.

"Thanks," she says. Underneath she's wearing a strapless shirt that just sits on her small breasts. I am still holding the bottom of the shirt and she looks down at my hands. I haven't let go and I don't want to. All I can think about is how I know she's not wearing a bra underneath. Her skin is smooth and pale and the shirt clings to her. It is so perfect and thin.

31

"I don't want any kids either," I say. I feel stupid for saying it. She's looking at me like I've got my lines all out of order. I might.

I still haven't let go. I grip the sides of her shirt tighter and I pull slowly downward. The elastic top catches on her nipples. I can see the soft pink skin right above them. I tug and the shirt falls down around her stomach. She has such small nipples. I touch them with the tips of my fingers and thumb.

"Kids ruin everything," she says. We do have the dialogue all wrong. I should be saying something about these breasts.

She turns me around, and takes hold of the front of my blouse. She gets hold of each side and then tears it open, buttons popping everywhere, the breeze suddenly on my own breasts. She pulls my pants down, just to my knees, just enough so her hand can reach between my thighs, and then she shoves me forward.

"I ought to slap that lawyer," she says. "Right in that smug face." I am on all fours, with my face in the pine needles, and she is pushing one finger into me, slowly. She pulls it all the way out. I can feel the finger's nearness. My body knows it's there, but it isn't touching. Then she pushes it in again, a little further than before. Something underground is rumbling. I can hear cars honking on the street nearby. "He said that the judge would like me better if I were a mother. I'd have a better chance."

"You should kill him instead," I say. "You could be a murderess." I love that word. Murderess.

"He's not worth it," she says.

But it would be worth it. Of course it would. I used to read about murderesses, hidden in the back of the library. The big book of murderesses. I read that book again and again. That was the first time I fell in love. Page 67. She killed her whole family in the middle of the day one Sunday afternoon. In her picture, she scowled.

My murderess.

This girl is no murderess, but she scowls. She has another finger at the mouth of my cunt now. Two fingers. She has a wet fingertip against my asshole and then everything is hot. She is breathing on me and I press my face harder against the pine needles.

I think of my own lawyer, of the condescending frown he must have given the judge when I didn't show. Her finger is inside my ass now. She breathes on me again. Oh, please touch me. No. Don't touch me yet. My lawyer frowns at the judge, and the judge frowns at my lawyer. The prosecutor frowns at everybody. The big church windows burst inward and my murderess is standing above the courtroom screaming. Guns are firing everywhere. She has her tongue on me now. It is too soon. It is perfect. She's licking all the way from my clit to my asshole. She licks so slowly and so firmly. Back and forth. She spends her time with each.

The courtroom is on fire, everyone is standing on their chairs. There is music playing and the air smells like pine needles. I have pine needles in my mouth, I am moaning and biting the ground, driving my teeth and tongue into the dirt while she fingers and tongues me.

My mouth is full of dirt. There's a sound in the brush, and I look over, expecting a man out walking his dog in the park, hiding in the bushes and watching the free show. But it isn't a man. It's an animal. It's so big.

She doesn't see, her tongue still working between my legs. The creature goes straight for her, and there is a sound like crisp lettuce being broken. Then I am on my back, trying to get out of the way, blood on the backs of my thighs, her finger still inside me.

patricia

I have a list of six names scrawled on a grocery pad, and in
block letters up top it says: "Geniuses to have sex with." Underneath, I've added: "(in order of sexiness)" but that's hard to do. I
hemmed and hawed and in the end I just listed them randomly,
boy girl boy girl boy boy.

Genius number one was "Richard Feynman (1918-1988)"
and his name's already crossed out. I took a red pen and drew a
little frowny face, too. Asshole.

Genius number two is "Patricia Highsmith (1921-1995)"
She's standing behind the counter over there, twenty one years
old, gaunt and fierce. There are pimples along one side of her
forehead, but when she turns everything is fine again. Her skin
on this side is smooth and perfect, like in the photographs I've
got up on my walls.

With Feynman, we made love after he'd already won the No-
bel Prize. That kind of success does something to a person in
bed. It was awful. But Pat hasn't even begun her first novel yet,
and I have a chance at the real her. The real Patricia Highsmith,

blemished, violent, brilliant. I want something from her, but I don't know what it is. I guess that means sex.

She's straightening the dolls on the shelf behind the counter. What do you say to someone you've stalked through time? Do you come here often? Can I buy you a drink?

She'll just say, "Thank you, no, I'm a lesbian. You shouldn't be here. This makes no sense. I'm long dead."

The note was a better idea, I think. It's taped to her jacket sleeve, a small green envelope with "Pat" written on the front. Inside there's nothing. What do you say? I wanted to just write "1995" on a slip of paper. I wanted to write a passage from *The Talented Mr. Ripley*. I wanted to write, "I'm not so ugly. What does it matter? It's just one night. Take me home." I'm sleeping in a park nearby. I've got no money here.

She's talking with a customer, smiling, and I'm thinking I should walk over and ask, "Haven't you ever wondered about the construction of a moral universe within the novel?" I'm thinking I could put my hand on her neck all easy, and say, "I'm at least as well-endowed as any woman. Give it a chance."

I thought being this close would let me see into her head a little better. It's worse, really. The zits have sort of driven home that she's a real person, more complex than the little snatches of interviews could possibly show. Before, I could believe I knew her, that I could see the passions that drove her characters, the fears that twisted the plots of her novels, but now I can see that's bullshit. It's written all over that side of her forehead.

There's a picture on the wall in my kitchen of Pat standing in a doorway, shadowed and naked, her skin perfect. My friends never want to have dinner over, it's always, "Let's eat out," or "Come over for pizza," and it's because I stare. What an amazing picture. I should have tried to find out what day that was taken. I should have shown up then.

The customer is still talking. He's ugly, balding, and I swear to god if he touches her elbow once more I am going over there. She's smiling even though I know that inside she's hating him, wishing he would go away, imagining some death for him, some completely justifiable murder. Does he show up in a novel? I try to remember.

Her hair looks nice. Maybe I should wait a few days to approach her, until the pimples have cleared up. It will distract me in bed. The customer looks over, meets my eyes. One of his ears is higher than the other, just a bit.

"Excuse me," he says, loud enough for everyone in the department to hear. "Is there something I can help you with?" Now I can see that he's got a name tag on, too. How long have I been standing here watching? Has it been twenty minutes? An hour? Both of them are looking at me, expectantly. "Are you waiting to be served?" he says, and I nod, looking at her.

She walks so strangely. I've never seen her move, her back up, her eyes on mine. Shit. Shit. Her name tag says, "Patricia," and I want to reach out and wet my fingers in her eyes. It doesn't feel right. She's looking through me. I turn and start walking away. In my head I beg her not to say anything. I don't want to hear her voice yet.

On the bench outside I think, will I end up in her journals? If we go to bed, will she write me down in cruel honest description? In fifty years, will I be mentioned in a biography? Will I be a brief detour on the road trip they paint of her psychosexual development as an artist, or a fork in the road? Will she come? Will she want me to want her to come, or will she want me to play indifference? Will she want me to come?

I find her later in the bar, drunk with her arm around a nervous looking girl from the university. The top button on her blouse is undone. I sit a few feet from them and I watch as the girl pulls free, as she looks around for her friends and takes off, drink in hand. Pat watches her walk away, bored. I take a deep breath. I stand.

In bed she tells a dirty joke. She forgets my name. She touches me and laughs about my ridiculousness. I tell her, "I've always loved your novels," and she laughs harder. In the end she comes, and doesn't care if I do or not. I ask, if she wants me to come and she points off to the bathroom and says it's none of her business what I do out of her bed. She says to clean up afterwards.

I want to lay down and cuddle, but she's having none of it. She's pouring herself a drink and looking at me differently. I have no idea what she's thinking. I say, "The individual has manifold shadows, all of which resemble him, and from time to time have equal claim to be the man himself," and she just sits there drinking. Have I got my dates wrong? Maybe she doesn't start reading Kierkegaard until '48 or '49. I start thinking that I should go, but this isn't right. I haven't come and I want to, I think it's important to come.

"Haven't you got somewhere to be?" she says, sounding annoyed. I want to say something perfect, something that cuts to the root of who she is, but also makes her want to make love with me again. I'm stammering in the doorway, foolish in my underwear.

"I... I like your cat," I tell her, and we're both dead quiet for almost a minute.

And then she smiles.

checkmate

It's only the second floor. With the right shoes, it wouldn't hurt to fall from that height. Cassie crawls out the window and along the ledge to the computer room. It isn't a very wide ledge, so she moves slowly. And when she gets close, she moves even slower.
She can see Carl's shoulders inside and she slows down because she doesn't want him to hear her. Carl moved his computer near the window a week ago, to hide whatever he was doing. Cassie figures porn.

She's got nothing against him watching porn and hiding it. She likes the idea. Everybody should have their secrets. She also likes the idea of sneaking out the window and watching him. She's going to masturbate on this ledge, watching Carl like a peeping tom.

But, inside, Carl isn't watching porn. He's playing online chess. Instead of nude bodies twisted under harsh lighting, the screen is a grid of black and white pieces and a square of text where he's chatting with his opponent.

Cassie's come all this way, though, and she can still pretend. She half-closes her eyes, so that the details fade out. She pictures pornography on the screen. She slides her hand down into the front of her pajamas, pushing under the elastic waistband of her panties. One of her legs sticks out over the edge.

In her head it's lesbian porn, the kind directed by men so that the girls are stuffed full of big fat dildos and they keep yelling things like, "I'm sorry I got an F, Daddy," even though there are no men in sight. So, when Carl reaches forward to type again and she sees his cock, it takes a moment for Cassie to realize that she hasn't imagined it.

He types something quickly and then puts his hand down onto his lap again. The angle is shit, but she catches another glimpse of his penis sticking up. His pants are open at the fly, but not pulled down. He has his fist wrapped around the shaft. There's no porn on the monitor, just the chat box. Cassie presses closer to the window, so she can read what's on the screen. His opponent is named "Checkmate_girl16" and Carl's online name is DOMINATOR.

Checkmate_girl16:	They're pink. I borrowed them from my friend. Mine were ripped.
DOMINATOR:	you rip them? you fall?
Checkmate_girl16:	I don't remember. I get too drunk on beer. I can't keep track of what happened. Someone else ripped them.
Checkmate_girl16:	That was a stupid move. I should have moved my bishop. Can I take that back?

DOMINATOR: maybe your boyfriend rip them?
                    he rip them off and fuck you
                    hard.

Carl's talking to a sixteen year old girl. Pervert! Cassie has a
stupid grin on her face. DOMINATOR? She had no idea at all
that he was into this. Was this what he thought about when they
fucked? She moves her fingertips slowly underneath her, the
back of her wrist presses into the ledge as she watches Carl and
starts to grind against her own hand.

She imagines Carl in one of those leather masks with a zipper
on the mouth. Those are terrifying and silly at the same time.
Imagining the mask on Carl startles her, though. She lets out a
little gasp and pushes her fingers harder into herself. She slides
them inside, then pulls them out, pressing them, wet, against her
asshole before sliding them back into her cunt.

She watches as Carl leans forward to type again. It's a long
message, and Cassie imagines what he's typing, the filthy things
he's promising to do to Checkmate_girl16. One of her fingers
stays in her ass, now, almost to the first knuckle, pulling against
the side, while her thumb strokes and touches the spot just above
where her vagina opens for her other fingers. Her whole hand is
moving. When Carl sits back from the keyboard, there is a new
message on the screen. Cassie strains her neck to see. She wants
to see the words, "Brutal," and, "Rough," and, "Fuck."

Checkmate_girl16:   My boyfriend would be too shy to
                     do that, I think. He's only
                     seventeen. I don't remember who
                     did it to me. Sometimes when I
                     am drinking I end up in the
                     country bar downtown, where
                     they don't ID me. I let men buy

me drinks and take me in the bathroom. I love to feel them inside me.

Carl isn't **DOMINATOR** at all. Cassie's hand starts moving again beneath her and, as she watches, another message appears on the screen, this one from Carl's opponent.

DOMINATOR: You are slut! Do you love to have cock in you? WHAT DO YOU DO FOR ME?

Carl leans forward to respond.

Checkmate_girl16:   I don't know. What would you do to ME if I was too drunk? Would you share me?

She wants to reach out her hand and tap on the window, right then, but she crawls backward to their bedroom window instead. Is this what he does while she's at work?

The next day, Cassie buys a bottle of wine on the way home from work. She stops at a small store with a display wall covered in dildos. She picks one, veined with thick ridges. Modeled after a real cock, but not too large. The clerk helps her pick out a harness, explains how it fits.

At home, Carl cooks dinner, and they eat and drink in silence. He has a second glass, and without asking Cassie pours him a third. After dinner, she leans down close and she puts her hand on his leg.

"I want to fuck you," she says. She kisses him roughly and pulls him into the bedroom, leaving the dishes on the table. Cassie pulls a pair of handcuffs out from under the pillow, and handcuffs Carl to the foot of the bed. She ties a blindfold around his eyes.

She kisses the very back of his neck, and then pushes his face into the blankets. Then she pulls out the new dildo from under the bed. She warms it up in her hands while Carl sits there, waiting, hard.

"Okay, he's ready," Cassie yells, like she's yelling to someone in the hall. She gets up quietly and pulls the door open fast. Carl looks over at the door, still blindfolded, confused. Cassie sneaks back to where she was sitting beside the bed, and continues to talk as though someone is there. "You can be rough if you want," Cassie says. "Just wear a condom." She pulls his pants down and begins to finger lube into his ass. She slaps him, and then again.

"Cassie?" Carl says, quietly. She doesn't answer. She slides her finger into him a little deeper, and he lets out a low moan. She has the dildo in her harness now and she rolls a condom down over the length. When she grabs his hips, she grabs them hard, so he doesn't recognize her touch. She puts the tip of her cock against his ass. Carl bites his lip as a stranger presses against him from behind.

She goes slowly and they still have to stop a few times for more lube. Cassie is still playing the part, slapping him hard, pretending to be a man, using Carl like a common whore. He writhes underneath her, and he yanks at the handcuffs and when they are done he says, really quietly, "Oh, Cassie, this was nice."

this is math

The man sits on Rose's couch too easily. He's used to making strange living rooms his home. She clears her throat and turns to the door.

"In here," she says.

She's not going to be intimidated by his notepad filled with numbers. There's nothing to numbers, no substance. It's all one through ten. She can count and she knows better than to be scared of some man who counts for a living.

He gets up and joins her at the table.

"This shouldn't take long," he tells her. "We'll just go over your expenses. Do you have your receipts?" He has a degree in accounting, she guesses, which he probably thinks is math. It isn't. The word counting is right there, inside it. They all think that counting is math.

Rose never got higher than a C- in high school math and that was good enough for the school boards and good enough for her. It wasn't math, either. He probably got an A. The first time she ever saw math, real math, was in that used bookstore, when she opened an old book and let her breath catch inside of her. The symbols were a maze on the page, an incantation. It was a coded message that sent electricity through her whole body and she put her own meaning into it, right there.

She stands up and motions for him to do the same.

"They're in my closet." she says and she meets his eyes in a way she knows looks good. In the closet, she pulls out the box of receipts, which is right on top. Then she pulls out the dirty magazines, one by one, setting them beside the door of the closet. He eyes them, but doesn't say anything. She moves slower, making her gestures more pronounced, exaggerated, like the plot points in a dirty movie. When she reaches the math book, the book of exercises, her fingers brush against the embossed cover. She turns and makes a pout and in a small voice, she says, "Do you know much about math?"

He smiles.

"I did my graduate studies in number theory," he says. It's unexpected, and there's suddenly a cold spot in her stomach, but she makes herself smile. "I like to think I'm pretty good." he says.

Rose pulls the book out, where he can see it.

"Then maybe you can help me," she says. She opens the book to the middle, and takes a marker from her pocket. She passes it to him, letting her fingers linger on his, and then pulls her hand away.

She rolls up her sleeve and there is an equation written there, in black. It's a series of symbols and numbers. There are Roman and Greek letters, all together, strung along a line that begins on the inside of her elbow. It is from a random page in the book. She has no idea what it means.

"That's not quite what I studied," he says, and she knows that this is the smile that he considers his charming smile. This is the one he pulls out in bars, or when he's being introduced to women he knows are single. She smiles back and touches the top button of her blouse with her other hand.

"If you can solve this one, there are more." she says and he looks again at the equation. He looks at it more seriously this time, taking her hand to hold the arm steady. She knows the answer, symbol for symbol, but has no idea what it means. She knows what it means to her. It's the first in a series of locks, lines of defense.

This is how it works. He'll struggle with the first question, but solve it. He'll solve the second and third, too. But they never make it past the fourth, and she sleeps with them anyway, because she feels bad. Because she's worried that nobody can make it past the fourth, or the fifth.

He reaches out for the book, but she shakes her head no and holds it closer to herself. He has a tight grin on his face.

"It's been a while," he says and she nods. There are symbols there that she'd never even seen in high school math and the farther beneath her clothes he gets, the less like counting the math would become. Eventually it would be nothing but magic to him and he would give up.

Only, he doesn't give up. He solves the first equation, writing the answer onto her palm, the soft tip of the marker moving with fast confidence. She pulls up the other sleeve, and he does it again, faster this time. He's smiling now and she undoes the front of her blouse.

"I hope you don't think this is going to make me any easier on your taxes," he laughs.

There are five equations on her chest, all drawn carefully with the black marker. She doesn't even have to look down to know that he's writing out the answers properly, symbol for symbol, perfect. His handwriting is like hers and he draws the symbols with the same care.

When he's done, he looks up from where he is knelt before her belly, and she nods. He undoes the first button of her jeans and begins to pull the zipper down.

"Give me the marker," she says. With both hands free, he pulls her pants to the ground and her legs are naked and un-marked. He reaches for the waistband of her panties, but Rose shakes her head.

She takes the cap off the marker and she begins to draw symbols on her legs, down one and up the other. This isn't an equation from the book, but one that just pours out of her. She's drawing from instinct, from her heart, and when she's done she passes the marker to the man. If he can't solve this one, there won't be any pity sex. She won't send him home with a consolation prize. This isn't counting anymore and he can't just turn to his calculator for the answer. This is math.

the green belt

I'm wearing the green belt because he can undo it with one hand. I'm wearing my black jeans because I can climb fences in them. Maybe I already did. I don't remember. I have a cut running from my wrist up around the outside of my arm to the elbow. It isn't deep, but there's dirt in it. It stings. It looks like a streak of black marker, precise.

I'm impatient.

Nine-fifteen on a Tuesday night, and I'm blurry-eyed drunk on the sidewalk with a broken boy. We look like assholes. I have an erection.

"Fuck that house," he says, lifting the bottle to point. "David used to live there," he says. "I went to school with him. He gave me this." He lifts his arm, showing me his elbow, but I don't see anything. "He had a baseball bat." He pauses and takes a drink. We stand and stare at the house, at the blue television light in the downstairs window. "I've never been so scared," he says, quieter. He takes another drink and then looks at me. "Hey," he says. "Is your arm still bleeding?"

"No," I say. "I'm good to go." I say it slow and careful. I say it obvious. He's still looking at the house, holding the bottle near his lips. A car rolls up the street and turns into a driveway a few houses down. I can hear a kid's voice. It's not even ten o'clock. I feel close to blacking out. The kid is whining. The mother says, "Shut up." Simple.

I take a drink from the bottle, then hand it back.

"Come on," he says, pulling me toward the back yard. He reaches over the fence and undoes the latch. I follow him into the grass and the dark. There's a window back here. I'm overwhelmed by something. Maybe fear. Mostly I'm thinking about fucking and then going home. I'm thinking about waffles for breakfast.

There's a light on in the kitchen of the house, but all we can see is a toaster, shining and chrome. All we can see is a microwave that blends into the wall. White. Tomorrow I will buy that hat.

This back yard is quiet enough. I take hold of the top button on his jeans and pull them open. He lifts the bottle again and I drop down in front of him.

"No," he says, but he doesn't stop me. I run my tongue up him, the very tip of my tongue. I take him inside my mouth. I suck his cock.

He pulls my hair sharply, and tilts my head back to look up at him. He pours the bottle on me, from above. My mouth is still open, but it splashes in my hair and across my cheeks. In my eyes. It splashes on my arm and everything is clear suddenly. The pain is bright.

He twists my hair in his hand and he yanks me back down on him and begins to thrust into my mouth. My eyes sting and my arm stings and when I look up at him he isn't even looking at me. He's staring at the house. Fuck it. I slide my hand down the front of my own pants, and run my fingers over the material of my underwear. I press slowly, moving all the way over my erection and then back up.

I am slow and then I am violent, like him.

I come first, and it's a struggle not to bite him. I bite a little and he comes. He comes in my mouth, thrusting faster and then so slowly that I forget we are moving. Everything is warm. He says quietly, "David."

edith

You haven't had time to write back and already I am writing you a second letter. I was taught to have better manners than this and I suppose this letter is evidence of how little I learned. I am not the proper young woman I could have been.

There are things I meant to say in my first letter, but I lost my nerve. First, you must have been confused to receive such an admiring letter about a story you have not yet published. Liz, the editor of the journal, is not to blame. She does not know I wrote to you or that I'm interested in you. She and I have never spoken about you. I found out about your story the old-fashioned way. I overheard.

At dinner, Liz called your story bizarre. She was talking to Sarah, another editor and a friend of hers, who seemed to have difficulty chewing with her mouth closed. Neither of them is ever terribly polite to me, so you'll have to excuse my unfavourable observations. I was eating my asparagus quietly, smiling whenever either of them made a joke. Once a week, we have family dinner. Liz insists on calling it "family dinner," though she and I are only roommates. She always invites friends. I never do.

This night, her guest was Sarah, a thin and gawkish brunette with manners best exemplified by her eating habits. Sarah consistently ignores me at dinner, unless there is wine. When drunk, she sneaks glances my way, and tries with very little subtlety to work my homosexuality into casual conversation. She has no romantic interest in me, as far as I know. It is the unfortunate combination of a child's curiosity and a journalist's ignorance of personal boundaries.

The two of them were going back and forth about the current issue of their literary journal, laughing over unsuitable submissions. They both thought it was very funny that an eighty year old woman might write pornography. They thought it was "cute." I was fascinated by the idea of you. I hadn't read your story. I knew nothing about you. But I spent the rest of that dinner lost in my thoughts, tuning out Liz and Sarah, imagining you.

It isn't quite accurate to say that I knew nothing about you. I knew you were eighty years old, four times my age, and still interested in sex. In my mind that had implications beyond those few spare facts. Writing pornographic literature is not an appropriate pastime for an eighty year old woman. In most people's minds, even having sex is inappropriate for an eighty year old woman and so you became inappropriate in my imagination. You spoke out of turn. You shocked people to take their measure, to put them off balance, but mostly for the sheer fun of it.

Also, because nobody is languidly inappropriate, you became very vivid, very animated. You laughed too loudly, and you gestured with your whole body. I imagined that you would have short white hair, and a bright face. Your eyes would be piercing and direct. Your lips would be hard and thin, but wet.

I remember, Sarah asked me a question as they were cleaning away the dinner plates and I looked at her blankly. I hadn't been listening. Liz rolled her eyes.

"Don't you have any homework you could be doing?" she asked.

I left them alone.

For the next few days, I thought about you in every spare moment. I thought about you while sitting in the cafeteria, while standing in line to renew my health plan. I decided, in the lobby of the student union building between classes, that perhaps you were not animated. You were reserved. You chose your words carefully. Or maybe your words poured onto the page, a sex-mad stream of consciousness. Your story would tell me more. I had to read it.

When Liz went out for the evening, I let myself into her bedroom. Liz is very conscious of her personal space. She would not have been pleased to come home and find me rooting through her desk. It was a risk, yes, but I had to know more about you. I stole your story and took it back to my bed. I sat down and turned on the small desk lamp. I read your story and I decided to write you a letter. Your address was on the first page of that manuscript. I couldn't resist.

In that first letter I didn't have the courage to ask you on a date. I wrote about how much I enjoyed your story and I said nothing else. Sometimes people are moved to voice their appreciation, but I have never understood that particular impulse. I was moved to voice my fascination, yes, but in the hopes that you would meet me. That was my motivation then, and that is my motivation now. Come out to dinner with me.

I have my outfit planned already. I will wear a simple black dress, like your story's protagonist wears at first. I am twenty-one years old and I program computers. I am studying at the university here in the city. Attached you will find a photograph of me. It is not a very flattering photograph. I look drunk and slightly out of control. But I chose this picture because I have my shirt pulled up. I want you to make no mistake about this. I am asking you to dinner because I would like to sleep with you.

Yours,

Ann.

Edith,

I should leave you alone. I wish I could. Another week has gone by with no response. I have read your story every night. I have read your story and enjoyed it the way you must have meant for it to be enjoyed. I masturbated to your story. Is that too graphic an admission? I wish I could shock you into meeting me.

But how could I shock someone who wrote, "I live to feel her fingers move inside of me like this. The bus makes another stop. A fat man climbs aboard, hauling himself up the stairs. I would kill him for one more moment with her fingers inside me. I don't have to. She gives me my moment for free. He lives because of her generosity. We all live because of her generosity."

I don't know what to do. I wish you would write back.

Ann.

Edith,

If the world were to end now, I might live forever, feeling this way.

This morning, sitting down to write to you, nothing seems quite real to me. For an hour I have been in my bed, beneath my covers, staring at the ceiling of this room, reliving last night. I remember the dress I wore, simple and black, soft against my skin. I tried to choose the perfect underwear. I did not have the courage to go without.

I was prepared for our evening date far too early and so I drank wine, sitting on the couch while Liz studied across from me in silence. When it was time, I slipped into my shoes and I was dizzy with excitement. I held tightly to the bar on the subway, repeating the restaurant's address in my head.

You were sitting calmly at the table, watching me. You were beautiful, Edith. Your dress was elegant and my first thought was frustration that my seat was so far from yours, on the other side of that table. But it afforded me a view of you, as you spoke.

You stood and offered your hand and I held it too long. I had not noticed the music that played throughout the restaurant until that moment, when your hand took mine.

Beyond that point, I don't know if I can provide an accurate accounting of my thoughts and feelings. I can certainly try. Everything about you was careful and calculated and strong. You talked so confidently. You were not the headstrong, shocking woman I had imagined before reading your story. Everyone in that restaurant was in awe of you. Your hair was white, the way I imagined. It was smart and sophisticated, like your dress. Your eyes were more blue than possible, perhaps because of the wine.

You asked me about computer programming. I stuttered.

But you smiled that confident smile again and you told me about working with the earliest computers, writing an article for the newspaper you would eventually own. When you described those machines, towering to fill whole rooms, making a noise to wake the devil, I felt like I was there with you. The idea of you in a room with that old machinery, pushing punch cards into the reader, writing notes in your notebook, it seems so perfect and right.

You told me about flying a small plane through the mountains. I sat there with nothing to say. I already knew everything I might say. I have never seen the mountains, unless you count the large rocky hill near where I grew up, or the ski slopes an hour out of town. I have never seen mountains the way you mean mountains, enormous, reaching up into the sky, peaked with snow. You paused and I might have told you that. I might have told you about how my father used to climb mountains and how every year he promised to eventually take us with him. It is a promise he still makes when the family is all together again. But I stayed quiet. I've heard my own stories before. Every new story out of your mouth was exciting and unexpected. I would have been a fool to speak.

Our skinny waiter bowed and fawned over you, as though you were someone's grandmother. He checked on us too often, asking, "Is everything alright, here? Is there anything I can do?" as though you were about to keel over. I wanted to tell him that you could snap him like a twig.

Instead, I put my hand on yours and I gave him the look, the lesbian look, the animal-crouched-over-her-family look, mixed with sex. This is mine. I will tear you apart.

He stepped back, still smiling politely.

I can tell you this, Edith. When you squeezed my hand in return, I knew I had done the right thing, writing to you. The waiter faded into the background, leaving us alone. I wanted you to tell me another story, but you watched me instead.

You asked me questions then, and I gave only short answers, certain you couldn't be interested. But you persisted. I babbled about the first girl I had ever kissed, Laura. I'm not sure that you were interested in how her room was decorated, or how strange we acted around one another after that kiss. I should have told the story better.

I wish I had asked you about your first kiss, Edith. But instead I babbled about university, about programming computers, about hiding from the lesbians at my school, because I don't like belonging to clubs.

You told me that a woman should be brave. I don't recall the context. You said, "A woman should be brave." Are you someone's grandmother? When was your first kiss? I should have told you, Edith, about the look on Laura's face after our kiss, half-shocked, but half-dreamy. I imagine I looked the same way when you kissed me last night. I died. You walked me to my cab and kissed me on the mouth, and I died.

I died and I am living forever.

Ann.

Edith,

My roommate Liz told me that I hide in my room. We finished dinner and I put away my dishes. I was on my way back to my bedroom and Liz said, "It's no wonder you don't have any friends."

Her theory, bless her concerned soul, is that I am "antisocial." She had a whole list of examples prepared. I never talk at the dinner table when she has guests over. She phrased it, "When we have guests over," though the guests are never mine. I never go dancing on Friday or Saturday nights, despite having been invited on two separate occasions by Liz herself. I wondered, as she listed these proofs of my anti-social tendencies, how long she had been preparing this list. It did not have the feel of a spur-of-the-moment conversation.

I held my tongue. I wanted to tell her about you, Edith, and about how I slipped out of my room last night, long after she had gone to sleep. I walked through the dark streets, and you met me down in the subway station, wearing a long black coat that suited you well. Light fell into that coat. You looked like a revolutionary.

Would Liz have worn that same smug smile on her lips if she had seen me, hand in hand with you, slipping past the security cameras, climbing past the gates? We disappeared down the walkway along the inside of that tunnel, and Liz has never done anything of the sort. You led me down thin metal platforms. We climbed down ladders, into deeper tunnels, down where the air tasted like dirt and oil and machinery.

There were switches there, and controls. You pushed me up against a box covered with grimy buttons, and you told me, "This is where you can have me." I was overcome. Behind us, a secret door opened and on the other side was the oldest computer I have ever seen. There were flashing tubes and blinking lights. It was like an old science fiction movie. Lightning shot from one part of this old relic to another. I was amazed. Everything was suddenly so overwhelming. The machine clattered. You pressed your lips to mine. Lightning, again.

Then you took my hand in yours and led me into the hidden room. You climbed backwards onto a table and pulled your dress up, exposing your panties. I slipped my finger under the waistband. These memories excite me. I hope you will excuse me if I slip and say something untoward. I am trying my best.

What did Liz do last night? She drank wine with her editor friends. They sat around our kitchen table and laughed about students who wrote predictable plots, embarrassing love scenes. I was underground, anti-social and lit by lightning, deafened by the insane rattle and shrieking of machines that had been antiques long before I was born. Your skin was so soft. I went down on my knees in front of you, resting my hands on the table top, and I kissed the skin on your legs. You lifted your dress higher. Your coat hung down to the floor. I kissed you and your skin was so thin and folded and soft. I said that already, didn't I? Soft. Soft. Soft.

Punch cards were spilling out onto the floor of the room and a man with an old scientist's lab coat came bustling in from a secret door. His hair was wiry and frazzled. He went right to the wall of computers, where he began flicking switches. The lights went out and the room was lit only by intermittent flashes of lightning. The lights came back on and you tensed up under my touch when you saw him.

"Don't mind me," he said. "Don't mind me one bit. I have to collect these calculations. Very important. Very important." He started scooping all the punch cards into his bag. I kissed you. I trailed my tongue from your knee to cunt. I pushed my tongue into you. Punch cards kept pouring out of the computer. I imagined the machine's insides, all gears and tubes and lights flashing. Edith, it was a wonderful second date.

Love,

Ann.

Edith,

How can I get your attention?

I read your story. I loved it. I want to meet you, but if you are not interested, please write to say so. This is my sixth letter and at this point, any response would do. Of course, a positive response would make me happiest. Come on a date with me. I'm not crazy. I want to sit in a restaurant with you. I won't hiss or growl at the waiter. I won't expect you to lead me to any hidden underground computer rooms. I just want to meet you, to hear your voice, to get to know you.

I sound like I'm writing greeting cards.

Tonight is one of those nights where you find yourself alone in your bedroom reading pornography. To be more accurate, it is one of those nights where I find myself alone in my bedroom reading pornography. Only, instead of arousal, it has conjured up a mixture of arousal and nostalgia. That is a dangerous combination.

Tonight is one of those nights where you think about calling old lovers to see how they are. Perhaps they want to meet up, right now, for coffee. Or perhaps they'd like to watch some television. Should you call? Will they be able to hear in your voice what you really want?

Tonight was worse than that, Edith. Tonight I went one step further and actually called. I picked up the telephone and dialled. I called Fiona, at one in the morning, making every effort to sound casual, to give the impression that one o'clock phone calls were nothing out of the ordinary for me.

"Oh, hello Fiona. How have things been?"

What is the matter with me? Fiona and I were together for less than a month. We met in a record store, shared a laugh over two young men who stood at the front of the store. They were very confident in their tight pants, talking knowledgeably at one another about influential but obscure bands. Fiona wore tight pants, too, though we never once spoke knowledgeably about anything obscure or influential. We hardly spoke at all.

Even our lovemaking was quiet. She would come over and we would watch television, sitting close together on the couch. We would move, slowly, closer and closer together, until our legs touched, until her hand rested on my knee, until her head rested on my shoulder. Then her hand would begin to move, first trailing her fingers gently, then squeezing my leg. I would run my fingers through her hair, then down onto her face. We never talked about this. When we talked on the phone, she said, "Want to watch TV tonight?" or, "Want to play video games again?"

We would make innocent plans, and one thing would lead to another. But then it stopped. She came over to play video games and we did not move closer and closer together. We sat and made small talk and laughed, the same as before. I tried moving closer on my own and when I was close enough to put my hand on her knee, she stood up for a glass of water.

I should not have called her tonight.

"Are you seeing anybody these days, Fiona? Oh? A boyfriend? Ha ha, well, if you ever find yourself missing the gentle touch of a woman. Oh, you know exactly what I'm talking about. What? No. No, I was only kidding. I'm sure you're very happy together, Fiona."

I tried to think of a subtle way to mention that I still think about her. But what do you say? There is no subtle way to mention you miss the curve of someone's ass.

When I touch myself, I sometimes think about Fiona, face down, bent over the coffee table of my old apartment, a video game paused on the television, her pants around her knees to expose the smooth skin of her raised ass. That was all I could think about, while I tried to make casual conversation on the phone at one o'clock. Her ass, and the way she used to writhe and moan into the carpet.

I should not have called her.

Nobody ever wants to talk about the good times.

And if you ever write to me, Edith, will you tell me that you have a boyfriend, too? Men don't live as long as women. I feel certain I could outwait him. I want you.

I want to make you writhe and moan into the pillow with your ass up. I don't care if you collect your things afterward without saying a word. I don't care if you slam the door.

Or I could moan for you, if you prefer. I could wail. I could call you daddy, or mommy, or Santa Claus. It is too late and I have had too much to drink. I wonder if you're awake. I wonder if you have nights like this.

Ann.

surprise

I got a haircut, short on the sides and chunky on top. I looked so different. It made me wish I wore glasses normally, because then I could have taken them off and I would have felt even more like Superman. At the bar I sat with my friends.

They didn't see her and I didn't point her out. Her dark hair was wet and short, sticking every which way. When she stood to go to the bar, her pants hugged her hips and her t-shirt was grey and tight. She had perfect breasts.

So I stood up to meet her. I leaned through the crowd at the bar so that my arm touched hers and I meant to say, "You're beautiful," but it came out just, "Beautiful."

"Get a new line," she said. She took her beer and started walking back to her friends. I caught up with her and touched her arm. She turned and shifted her weight, waiting expectantly. "Alright," she said. "One more try. You've never seen anyone with eyes as pretty as mine? Don't you know me from somewhere?"

"I want to pull your shirt up over your face," I said. "and leave it like that, so that your chest is bare and your face and arms are covered. I want to kiss you through the shirt and have your makeup stain it. I want to pull your pants to your knees and your panties half that distance. I want to open the bathroom stall while you're blind and full with my fingers, so another man walks in and sees you blindfolded."

She didn't say anything. She took a sip of her beer and looked me up and down. Then she smiled. She had a beautiful smile. If this were a toothpaste commercial, I'd say her teeth were luminous.

"What's your name?" she said.

In the bathroom I did pull her shirt up over her face, but her makeup didn't stain it. Her breasts were soft in my hands, and I trailed my fingertips over her skin. I ran them across her nipples, then back again, feeling the flesh swell as they hardened. Small hard bumps ran scattered around the nipples, like Braille. She kissed me through her shirt, hard, and I reached down to unfasten her belt.

When I let go of her t-shirt to pull her pants down, she used the freedom to pull her shirt the rest of the way off. She took me by the hair and pulled my head down to where her legs were opening. I kissed her stomach and her belly button and that invisible downy trail of hair. My tongue ran along the top of her pubic hair, and then pressed down through her cunt. It parted the hair and found the dry outer part of her and pulled her open to where she was wet. My lips and tongue and nose got wet with her while she pulled my hair, pushed me around, shook me side to side and up and down on her while the tip of my tongue fought to find just the right motion, something rhythmic and correct.

She shoved me back against my side of the stall, and lifted my shirt up over my face. She used it to hold my arms above me, but I could see through. I reached my hand out for the stall door, and she caught it.

"What are you doing?" she said.

"Opening the door," I said, and she shook her head. She lifted my arm back above me.

"No," she said. "I didn't like that part of your idea."

She ran her tongue over my chest, through the small patch of hair in the middle, to the nipple on the right. She ran the tip around and then around the nipple again. She kissed it, then opened her mouth wider and took the whole nipple and sucked, then bit, and then moved on. She took my hands and kissed her way down my stomach. She put my hands in her hair, made fists of them, and used them to press her face against my pants. I was hard now, constricted by my jeans. I took her hair in fists and ground against her face. I pulled her hair hard and drove my zipper into the soft quiet flesh of her lips and eyes and cheeks.

"Wait," she said. "Wait, this is boring."

I was still pulling her hair, grinding my dick into her mouth as she spoke.

"What?" I said.

"This is boring." She pulled away from my jeans and took my hands out of her hair and sat back against the wall of the bathroom stall. Her left breast had a line from the seam of my pant leg, just beside the nipple. "I thought this was going to be new, exciting, but you're just going to fuck my face. Any one of those men out there could skull fuck me. I thought you were going to surprise me, startle me."

I made myself look disappointed, and I made my voice really quiet. I muttered something, and she leaned forward to hear.

"What?" she said, and I let my lower lip shake like I was about to cry. When she rolled her eyes and turned away, I grabbed her shoulders and hollered as loudly as I could:

"Boogidy-boo!" I yelled and she screamed in shock. After that, she gave me her phone number and kissed me on the mouth. She made me promise to call her the next day. Her birthday.

Walking home, I thought about her mouth through the fabric of her t-shirt. I thought about her nipples and the rough way she had forced my mouth down on her. I thought about my bed at home and my stereo playing quietly while I masturbated. It was the beer and arousal combined, I think, that made me climb into the bushes between two downtown office buildings.

There were flowers here and the dirt I laid my head on was freshly turned. It smelled like worms and grass and roses. I couldn't see the stars, because of the lights shining down, but I could hear the laughter of other drunks in the streets around me and that was good enough.

I undid my belt, opened my pants, pulled myself free. My hands were wet and grimy with mud, from climbing through the bushes, and it was cool against my cock. I was covered in dirt, scratched from the bushes, yellow light from above. I thought about her and realized that she hadn't even told me her name. Just given me her phone number and squeezed me one last time through my pants before she left.

It didn't take me long to reach that point where you have to slow down, where you can feel it rising inside of you and you realize that you don't know where you're going to put the come. I looked around for a big leaf or flower, something to take the place of tissue, but found nothing. So I climbed to my knees. I leaned forward with my left hand sunk in the mud and my right hand moving faster and faster, I thought about her tongue licking the very inside part of my ear, and I thought about her writing out her phone number on that scrap of paper and I came on the ground.

Then I re-zipped, re-buckled, and walked home. The shirt was caked in mud. In my mirror I looked more like Superman than ever before. I called the office, drunk, filthy, and left a message saying that I was sick. I wouldn't be in. I didn't know how long. I fell asleep on the floor in my clothes.

The next day was her birthday. The rain stopped by the time I left my house, and halfway to the address she'd given me, I found an old typewriter out by the curb with someone's garbage. It seemed perfect for her and I picked it up without giving it a second thought. It was an old travel typewriter, like a heavy suitcase. The sort of thing Clark Kent would carry.

She opened her door and I swung the typewriter up and into her stomach. The weight of it knocked her backwards, pulled me by the hand on top of her. She let her breath out and I fumbled with the clasp on the typewriter and opened the case. I pulled the machine free, set it on her breasts. Keys were missing and there was ink and grime crumbling onto her. I was hard.

The typewriter was between her face and me. She reached around it to where she knew my belt was. She pulled at it roughly while I began to type. The '4' stuck. She got me in her hand. The '8' stuck. Through the typewriter I could see her breasts. The '8' stuck again. I lifted the machine and dropped it on her hard. She gasped, and tears started running down the sides of her face from the corners of her eyes. I lifted the typewriter again and suddenly it was a giant needle in my hand. Her eyes went wide. She was thinking I might drive the needle deep into her heart and kill her. Her nipples were hard like my cock in her hand.

Instead, I stuck the needle into a giant balloon that was floating by. It burst. She screamed at the sound. There was confetti everywhere. I burst another balloon and she screamed again. But it was a delighted shriek. She was laughing. I popped another balloon and she clapped her hands. She kissed my penis. I surprised her.

the meteor shower

Is this really where I want to be? Stacking printer paper in an office supply store? Seriously? For how much longer? We're all going to die. Death is taking another lick of my lollipop, and God only knows how many licks it takes before he gets frustrated and just bites into it.

So, I'm quitting. Happy birthday to me. I'm almost thirty. The work isn't terrible. But it's never the actual work that's terrible, is it? It's the customers. Jesus fuck — the customers.

This one walks over and sets the printer paper down, already staring at the little screen where the price appears.

"That's not the right price," the customer says and he slaps down a flyer that's opened to a picture of printer paper. He's jabbing at it.

"Well, that's last week's flyer, sir." I say.

"Excuse me?"

"That's an outdated flyer. We have copies of the new flyer, here, if you like."

"You sent me this flyer, and I drove all the way downtown because of the price promised right here." He jabs. "Now if you're just going to give me more faggot excuses, I'd like to speak to your manager."

Classy. So, I pick up the phone and I call my manager, Wallace. Then the customer and I wait in silence. He's probably sixty years old. Dressed nice, but not fancy. He has a shirt and tie, but no blazer. And it's a shirt that's been worn again and again. There are no crisp corners. A working man! Salt of the earth.

"How can I help you, sir?" Wallace says, coming behind the cash register with me, smiling at the customer. And the customer is nicer now. Of course he is. I watch while he explains the issue politely. He shows Wallace the flyer. Wallace hits a few buttons on the keyboard and everyone's happy. The customer gets the discount he wants.

It's always the people who are paid the least who have to take the most shit. Otherwise Captain Angry there to go buy his five-dollar printer paper at another establishment.

When he's gone, I turn to Wallace.

"That guy called me a faggot," I say and Wallace claps me on the shoulder warmly. He's a nice guy, I think. Not the brightest guy in the world, but mostly good. I get a bit uncomfortable when he talks about women, like, he's not really talking about people. But in general, Wallace means well.

"Don't take it personally," Wallace says. "Everybody gets what they deserve eventually. In his next life, that guy'll probably come back as a faggot himself." Wallace walks off, and I'm left standing there holding the receipt for one packet of printer paper. That doesn't make me feel better at all.

Wallace wouldn't have said it if he knew I slept with men. I know that. He's not a mean guy. Just stupid. Oh, so stupid. I stand behind the counter and I ring through people's orders, just waiting for one of them to say something.

By lunch time, I can feel a pressure behind my right eye that I am certain is my anger. It keeps on building and building until I don't know what to do with it.

In the faggot lunch room, Wallace is laughing with Mike, watching the faggot TV. I've been standing behind that cash register all day, angry. I haven't been able to think of anything faggot else, and I bet if I fucking faggot asked him right faggot now, he wouldn't be able to even tell me what he said. Long forgotten. Unimportant.

Anger isn't making me feel better. But you know what does make me feel a little bit better? Sexual harassment. The look on Wallace's face when I say, "Jesus, Wallace. You been working out? Your ass looks amazing today." Just a flash of surprise and confusion. A bit of shame. And then I'm gone, back up the stairs to my cash register.

I'm smiling now. I feel good, less helpless. I wonder if this is why straight men sexually harass women, to prove to themselves that they have power. They get yelled at by their own bosses and head back to the office to take it out on their secretaries. Hey, Janet, your tits look good in that top.

Later that afternoon, when Wallace is helping some guy pick a printer, I walk past him again, and this time I clap him on the shoulder and look pointedly down at his crotch.

"Come on, Wallace. Hide your erection, will you?"

"What?"

"It's impolite to walk around with candy unless you're gonna share."

I feel like a little kid, pissing on the bully's gym clothes. Sure, there are probably better ways to handle this, but I can't think of any. It's better to make it a joke. And it is a joke, isn't it?

I get off work earlier than Clay does, so I usually walk down and meet him at the casino. Clay has birthday plans for me tonight. A surprise. I'm leaning back against the hood of his car when he comes out.

He's still in his uniform, his security badge yellow under the parking garage lights. He looks good in that uniform. He looks dangerous. I have a bit of a weakness for dangerous-looking men.

I kiss him hello, then in the car I tell him about the customer,and about Wallace. But it's my birthday and mostly I want to talk about something else.

"What're we doing tonight?" I say and Clay smiles.

"Tonight, sir, there's a meteor shower," he says. "I don't know if you heard. It's kind of a big deal. We're going to go out to the country, where there are no streetlights, and were going to watch the sky fall." This is Clay's birthday surprise for me. It's hard to believe he even remembers the meteor shower. He's got no interest in anything like this, but I must have gone on about it one too many times, my voice all earnest, waving my hands in the air while I talked.

Clay gets excited about things, too. It's one of the things I love about him. He gets an idea in his head and it lights him up. There's not a cynical bone in his body; everything is fun. Everything's an adventure. It doesn't matter what the plan is. He has dozens of plans. Let's go to the movie on Tuesday. Let's go to China. Let's learn how to leave no trace at all in the world's databases and let's live off the grid. Let's learn to knife fight. We saw an ad about that. Learn to knife fight using training methods developed for Russian Special Forces. The flyer ended with the ominous, "You don't win a knife fight. You survive." There is always more room in our lives for something so deadly serious.

And Clay's enthusiasm is infectious. Now he's talking about Wallace again. He wants to come into the store wearing a leather vest. I have no idea where Clay would even find a leather vest. He wants to wear a big fake cop moustache. A disguise. Wallace has never seen him, which makes me feel weird, now that we've said it out loud. Clay's never been into the store. I've never been into the casino, either.

"I'll seem like just any other customer," Clay says. "Oh this is going to be brilliant," He's repeating himself now. This is how you know when he's really excited. He goes around in circles, and the idea is more exciting to him every time. He wants to get his friends to do it, too. Every queer he knows. Go in and blow Wallace kisses. Pat Wallace's ass affectionately after he's been helpful. Ask Wallace for his phone number.

When Clay's around, I feel like I'm more exciting, too. That's a good quality to have in a gentleman friend. I come up with plans of my own for us. Let's try to befriend the squirrels that live in the walls and attic. Let's go get some candy and stay up all night watching horror movies. Let's sleep over in a graveyard, so the dead can visit us in our dreams.

I don't fall in love very easily. It takes a long time and then, when I have fallen in love, I'm still not sure. I'm suspicious of myself. What if tomorrow I don't feel the same? I have to wait, to be sure. And I wait and wait. I think I might be at that stage with Clay. I've been waiting for a while now. I have dreams about telling him.

We drop the car back at the apartment and unlock our bikes. I love biking in the dark. I didn't think I'd get a chance to see the meteor shower tonight. I thought for sure he'd take me out to dinner or to some movie. Watching a meteor shower is amazing because to the human eye it just looks like dozens of little moving points of light. Thin streaks of light. Except they aren't. They're chunks of debris falling to earth. Fast and burning and where do they all come from? I'm not sure. They're little bits of something else.

Space always makes me think of infinity. The universe just keeps going and going and, when I think about it, it actually feels like my thoughts have to get bigger to understand. And then I get scared.

We bike out to the dark and find a perfect spot. We're in a field with a hill blocking the streetlight from the road, the best place for us to stretch out and watch the sky fall. We lay down side by side on the grass and dirt, watching the sky. Beside me, Clay says, "There!" and I see it too, the first streak of thin light.

We watch for a while, until I get scared thinking about the yawning void of space and the maddening smallness of our solar system in it and the smallness of our planet in that solar system and of my own voice in the dark and I almost say, "I love you," right then and there, but instead I pull him on top of me.

I like having his weight on me. I like the feel of his breath against my cheek and I like the feeling of being trapped, too. Pinned down. He kisses me and smiles, then tries to roll off me. I hold onto him tightly.

He pins my wrists to the dirt. He stretches me out so my belly's exposed and he kisses my neck. He puts his mouth right up against my ear and says, "Nobody can hear you out here. Cry for help all you want." And I struggle against his grip. He pins my wrists with one hand and with the other he pulls my belt open, shoves his hand down to wrap cool around my cock and I say, "No." And I try to pull free.

We forget all about watching the stars. He kisses me and I struggle against him just enough. "Let's move," he says. There's a tree here. We stand up and we kiss in the moonlight with the stars falling and no cars anywhere and oh it's all very perfect and romantic and all I can think about is I want him inside me. I want him to press his finger inside me.

He pushes me against the tree. I spin us so that he's against the tree and I put his hand in my hair and make a fist of it. He's smiling. He forces me down to my knees and I squeeze the front of his pants. Gripping a cock through them that isn't fully erect yet, but doesn't really need to be. I pull at the button.

I open my mouth, looking up at him, and he takes my hair in both his fists and shoves my face down on his cock. My lips are forced open. Then further. I'm still struggling, my hands waving helplessly in the air.

He's hard now. I make a choking sound as he reaches the back of my throat and I struggle. He pulls my head back to let me gasp for air and to force me to look up at him. He spits on me. His spit is thick on my face, and he says "Whore." He shoves me down on his cock again, fucks my face while I dig my fingers in the bark of the tree, the zipper of his pants cutting against my lips and cheek, again and again. Then my hand is up his shirt, pulling at his nipple and leaving streaks of dirt on his chest while he uses my mouth. Then he pauses.

"Is this okay?" he says, looking down, and I can only nod. Yes.

I want him to come on the ground here in front of me, or to come across my lips. I want him to push my face into the dirt and pull my pants roughly down just far enough so he can get at my asshole. My knees are wet and cold through my pants.

Clay pulls me back by the hair and forces me to look up at him again.

"My turn!" he says.

And so I twist his arm behind his back and push him against the tree with his shirt pulled up. The bark is digging into his chest, and I've got his pants pulled down so I can get at him. My free hand is wet with my own spit, my finger pushing at his asshole. I use my body to hold his arm twisted between us. My teeth are tearing at the condom wrapper. I wrap my hand around his throat while I enter him. "If you make one sound, I'll kill you," I whisper in his ear.

When I come, I panic a bit, because I can suddenly see everything. I have my hand around his throat and I feel like I am just returning into my senses. Did we go too far? But Clay reaches up and kisses me on the cheek and then on my mouth and he says, "You're beautiful."

77

Afterward, we watch the night sky, still half-naked. His chest hair is soft and I rest my head on him. The dirt and twigs are digging into the skin of my hip. My pants are still around my ankles. This is so quiet and would be such a perfect time to say, "I love you." But you can't say something like that just because the moment is right. It's too seductive, having the moment be perfect. I would worry that I said it just because it seemed like the right time. The stars keep falling.

"It makes me nervous," I tell him. One after another after another the streaks of light appear and vanish. "It goes on forever." I sound stupid. Chunks of burning rock from God knows where, raining down on us. Rocks that are older than our whole solar system. And when our sun explodes and we are all destroyed, we'll be rocks and chunks of I am not sure what. Maybe we'll rain down on somewhere else.

On the bike ride home, we keep making wide slow turns from one side of the road to the other in the dark. We talk about Halloween, which is soon. I say maybe tomorrow night we should go climbing trees in the neighbourhoods we grew up in and Clay says maybe we could learn how to fight with our bare hands.

Everyone should be able to kill a man with just their thumb. We could be ready for anything. There are whole martial arts devoted to just disarming someone. Just disabling them and getting away, Clay tells me. He knows just what I want to hear. My lips are raw and they taste a bit like blood and dirt and this is a perfect birthday.

calculator

At fifteen, I was caught with half a carton of rotten eggs in the woods. They knew it was me right away. I wasn't wearing a mask. Halloween was about being horrible, not just pretending.

The police never pressed charges. The man who arrested me knew my father from downtown. He sat down beside me in the back seat of the cruiser and rested his thin hand on my leg and said, "This is no way for a kid to behave."

At home, my mother took me upstairs to my room and laid into me with a wooden spoon. "You think you're too old for this?" And then I waited in the dark for hours. I waited until they were asleep and then I opened my bedroom window and I dropped from the second floor to the ground.

I landed on my ankle funny and limped to the garage for a weapon. A tire iron. There's a special way that a tire iron feels in your hand when you know what it's for. And I knew exactly what a tire iron was for. I broke sixteen car windows before dawn.

My hands were cold and shaking when I put the tire iron back and snuck back inside. At breakfast, I acted as surprised as my mother that the ankle was broken.

My father offered to pay for law school, if and when I got to be law school aged. I studied math instead, worked weekends. I kept breaking glass because I liked breaking glass. Baseball bats and wine bottles in the woods.

A sales clerk caught me with my hand down the front of my pants in the personal finance section of an office supply store. She turned bright red and I almost dropped the calculator I was holding. It had two lines of display, and a multi-level undo function.

I pressed the buttons on the calculator in sequence, exploring its functions, admiring the second display line, the speed of its calculations and the utility of its error control functions. I lost track of my surroundings. I slid my hand down the waist of my jeans and a fifty year old woman in a bright red vest was suddenly at the end of the aisle snorting at me.

Tuesday night in an office supply store, fingering myself. The woman spun and marched off. I wanted to run, but I wanted that calculator, too. I needed it. I wanted to take it home with me. Anyway, there were no cameras on the calculators. The cameras all pointed to laptops and ink cartridges. There was no evidence. It was her word against mine.

The only evidence was easily handled. I set the calculator on the shelf carefully and turned and walked through the bright, clean aisles toward the back of the store. The clerks that I passed smiled politely at me. They hadn't heard. They would.

At the back of the store I entered the bathroom and I ran my hands under warm water. I soaped them with a squirt of the pink pearl soap. I washed the soap away and then I soaped them again.

The calculator cost me sixty-five dollars at the front cash. Washing my hands had given the old woman plenty of time to spread the word. I paid in cash and smiled at the nervous girl behind the cash.

Outside, I sat in my car and took my knife to the packaging. I cut into the plastic again and again, until the calculator sat in my palm. Then I pressed the pad of my thumb against the shiny black ON button. The number zero appeared and already the world around me was beginning to fade.

I sat hunched forward in the parking lot of that store, my fingers on the plastic squares of the calculator, my other hand down the front of my pants. I had to concentrate. It was difficult, entering numbers and formulas with one hand and circling and stopping and circling again with the other. It was the perfect form of concentration.

When my legs began to shake, I pulled my hand out from my pants and I pulled them down to my knees. The skin on my leg pressed against the door of the car. I set the calculator against my cunt, so that the hard corner of the device pressed into just the right spot, and the cool plastic edge ran through the soft skin just right. I spat on my hand to make the plastic wet. I moved the calculator back and forth, pressing with the corner and then I reached for the knife.

I took the knife blade and pressed it into the fissure where the two halves of the calculator's casing met. I continued to press the calculator into me, moving it slower now, my thumb reaching for the function keys. I ran the knife to the top corner and twisted it, like I was opening an oyster. The casing cracked. I moved the knife to the lower corner.

My legs were shaking more and more. I was thinking one and one hundred thousand. I was thinking compound interest and multi-level undo functions. Two level display. I cracked the lower corner, and the calculator opened.

I leaned forward as I came and looked inside. I put the knife down and I ran my fingers, wet, over the circuitry of the calculator. There were no sparks. There was no hiss. The circuit board was flat, with sharp points, and it was slick under my fingers.

I leaned back into my seat and left my hand resting on the exposed and ruined insides of the calculator. My breathing came easily and I felt as though I could sleep right there in the parking lot. I don't know how long I stayed like that, listening to the passing traffic and the calm of my breathing.